This Peppa Pig book
belongs to

....

LADYBIRD BOOKS

UK | USA | Canada | Ireland | Australia
India | New Zealand | South Africa

Ladybird Books is part of the Penguin Random House group of companies
whose addresses can be found at global.penguinrandomhouse.com.
www.penguin.co.uk   www.puffin.co.uk   www.ladybird.co.uk

Penguin
Random House
UK

First published 2016
001

Printed in China

A CIP catalogue record for this book is available from the British Library
ISBN: 978-0-241-25166-9

All correspondence to:
Ladybird Books, Penguin Random House Children's,
80 Strand, London, WC2R 0RL

Contents

Peppa's Story . . .

Once upon a time, there was a lovely piggy named Peppa.

She lived in a beautiful house on top of a hill . . .

Snort!

with her little brother George . . .

Oink!

. . . and their mummy and daddy.

Colour in the pictures as you read Peppa's story, then draw a picture of yourself with your family here.

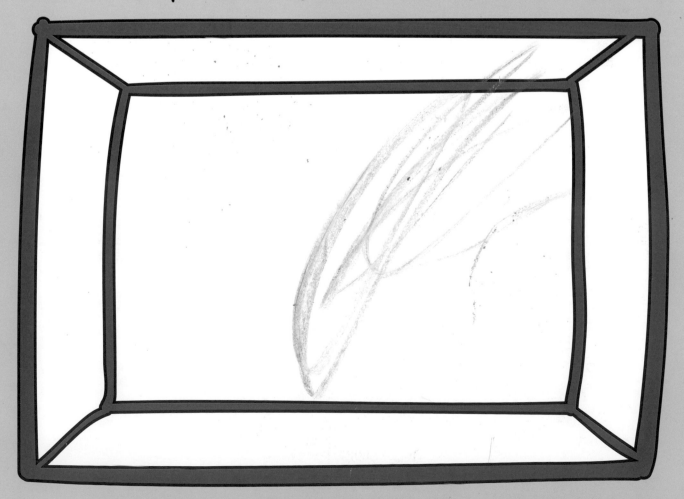

Peppa and George liked . . .

Oink!

playing together . . .

going for trips in
their little red car . . .

Snort!

having fun with their friends . . .

reading stories . . .

and dressing up.

But MOST of all they liked . . .

JUMPING IN MUDDY PUDDLES!

Splash!

Squelch!

Draw yourself jumping in muddy puddles with Peppa and George!

Story Time
Pirate Treasure

Peppa and her friends have dressed up as pirates.
Danny Dog is on board his pirate ship. "Are you ready to play?" he asks.
"Yes, we arrrrrgh!" everyone cheers in their best pirate voices.

This is our treasure chest.

Let's find some treasure to put in it.

Pedro Pony guards the pirate ship, while Danny, Peppa, Suzy Sheep and Freddy Fox search for treasure.

First, Danny finds a pine cone. "Treasure! Woof!" he barks.
Then Peppa finds a shell, Suzy finds some rope, and Freddy finds a pebble.
Everyone loves playing pirates and searching for treasure!

Meanwhile, back at the pirate ship, Pedro has taken off his glasses and
fallen asleep . . .

"BOO!" cry the pirates, creeping up on Pedro and waking him up.
"Oh!" gasps Pedro, surprised. "Sorry."
"We've got treasure to put in the treasure chest," says Peppa, showing Pedro.
Everyone puts their treasure in the chest.

Pedro guards the ship again, while the rest of the pirates head off to find
a place to bury the treasure.
Over a hill and round a little bush they go . . .

"Let's bury it here!" cheers Danny.
Freddy digs a hole. Danny puts the treasure chest inside and covers it with soil.
"How will we know where we've buried it?" asks Suzy.
"Let's make a treasure map!" says Peppa.

Peppa draws a treasure map. "Over the hill, round the little bush and
'X' marks the spot!"
Danny draws an 'X' on the ground to mark where the treasure is buried,
and the pirates head back to their ship.

When they get back, Mummy Pony arrives to collect Pedro.
"Stop!" shouts Pedro, guarding the ship. "Who goes there?"
"I'm your mummy," says Mummy Pony. "Where are your glasses, Pedro?"
"Oh no," says Pedro. "I think I put them in the buried treasure chest."

"We can find them with our treasure map!" cheers Peppa.
Mummy Pony uses Peppa's map to find the buried treasure.
"Over the hill, round the little bush . . . and 'X' marks the spot," says Peppa.

Peppa's map leads them straight to the treasure.
After Freddy digs it up, Pedro looks at it very closely . . . "My glasses!" he cries.
"Hurraaaaaahhh!" everyone cheers.

Hurraaaaaahhh!

"Treasure maps are very useful," says Peppa.
"Especially for finding glasses if you accidentally bury them!" adds Pedro.
"Ha, ha, ha!" everyone laughs. "Hurraaaaaahhh!"

Pirate Dress-up

Arrrrr! Peppa, Danny and their friends love dressing up as pirates! Can you spot the odd one out in each row?

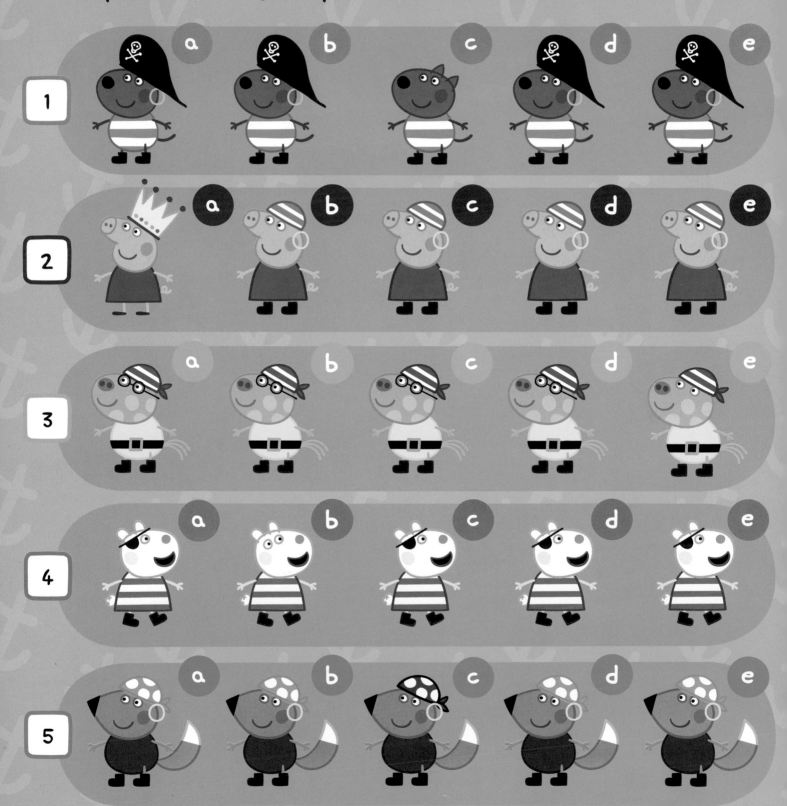

Answers: 1. c, 2. a, 3. e, 4. b, 5. c

Ahoy There, Me Hearties!

Use the numbers to help you colour in the picture of Peppa and her pirate mateys!

17

Treasure Hunt

Help Pirate Peppa and Pirate Danny follow the map to find the treasure. Draw an 'X' to mark the spot where you find it!

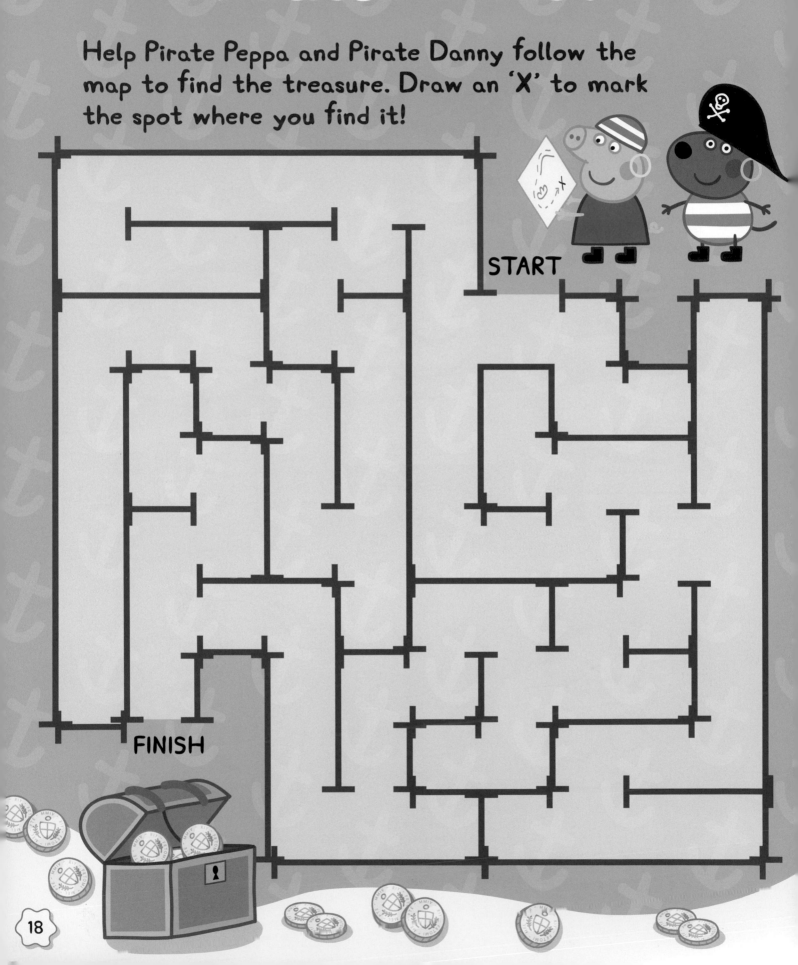

START

FINISH

Booty!

Booty is another name for treasure. What would you put in your treasure chest? Draw it here.

The Search for Pedro Pony's Glasses

Oh dear, now Pedro has lost his glasses at Danny's pirate party! Can you find them in the big picture?

20

What else can you spot?
Tick the boxes as you find each object.

Answer: Pedro's glasses are on the steamship picture frame.

21

Secret Message

Look at Peppa's secret message to you. Each letter has been replaced with a picture that starts with that letter. Use the pictures to work out the letters and spell out the message.

Answer: Peppa's secret message is 'hello!'

Spot the Difference

Yummy! Take a close look at these two pictures of Peppa and her family eating pizza on holiday. Can you spot five differences in the second picture?

Answers: 1. The umbrella has changed colour. 2. The last slice of pizza has moved to Daddy Pig's hat! 3. The sun has disappeared. 4. The chef has lost his moustache. 5. Peppa is wearing a chef's hat.

Story Time
Naughty Tortoise

It's autumn time, and Tiddles the tortoise is going to sleep for the winter.
But Tiddles isn't sleepy, so he has run away and climbed a tree!
"How are we going to rescue him?" asks Peppa.
"I'll ring the fire brigade," replies Dr Hamster.

"STAND CLEAR!" shouts Mummy Elephant when the fire engine arrives.
She puts the ladder against the tree and Mummy Cow starts to climb up
towards Tiddles.

Mummy Cow reaches the top of the ladder, but Tiddles climbs higher!
"Come here, you little pickle!" calls Mummy Cow.
"Be careful, Mummy Cow!" shouts Mummy Elephant.
But Mummy Cow climbs on to a branch and gets stuck.
Cows are not very good at climbing trees.

"HANG ON!" cries Mummy Elephant. "I'M COMING UP!"
Mummy Elephant climbs on to a different branch and she gets stuck, too!
Elephants are not very good at climbing trees either.

"What are we going to do now?" asks Peppa.
"I'll call another rescue service," says Dr Hamster. "Grandad Dog's breakdown truck!"

"Hmm," says Grandad Dog when he arrives. "How do you get tortoises out of trees? Shall I climb up?"
"Yes, please," replies Dr Hamster.
Grandad Dog climbs up on to the first branch in the tree.

"Oh," says Grandad Dog. "I seem to be stuck!"
Dogs are not very good at climbing trees either.
"Now what are we going to do?" asks Peppa.
"We'll have to call the highest rescue service in the land!" replies Dr Hamster.

Miss Rabbit arrives in her rescue helicopter.
"Hello, everyone!" she calls down. "Now, let's rescue this tortoise!"
Miss Rabbit puts her helicopter on autopilot and climbs down the ladder
to the tree.

"Got you, you little rascal," says Miss Rabbit, reaching out and grabbing
Tiddles from the top of the tree.
Then she carries him safely down to the ground.

"Thank you for saving my Tiddles, Miss Rabbit," says Dr Hamster.
"No problem, ma'am!" replies Miss Rabbit. Then she climbs back up the
ladder to rescue Mummy Elephant, Mummy Cow and Grandad Dog.
"Thank you for saving us, too!" they cry.
"Just doing my job!" replies Miss Rabbit. "Goodbye, everyone!"

"What a naughty tortoise you are!" says Dr Hamster.

"YAWN!" yawns Tiddles.

"Oh good, now you're sleepy," says Dr Hamster. "Back in your box you go."

"Sleep well, Tiddles!" cries Peppa.

Tiddles has gone to sleep for the winter and will wake again in the springtime.

"Shhh!" whispers Peppa. Everyone giggles, very quietly!

Climb the Ladder!

Tiddles is stuck in the tree again. Challenge a friend to see who can reach him first by playing this colouring game.

What to do:

Take it in turns to roll a dice and move up the ladder the number of rungs shown on the dice.

Colour in the ladder rungs as you go. The first player to get to the top wins.

Leafy Trail

Follow the lines of leaves to find the one that leads to Tiddles.

a

b

c

Colour the Seasons

Tortoises like Tiddles sleep all winter and wake up when it's warm in the spring. Colour in these pictures. Can you guess which season is shown in each one? Spring, summer, autumn or winter?

a

b

c

d

Noisy Traffic

Colour in the pictures of these vehicles.
What different sounds do they make?

How many vehicles are there all together?

How many carriages does the train have?

Answers: There are four vehicles. The train has two carriages.

Little Creatures

Choose the right letter sounds
to finish these animal words.

w   b   ee   f

Peppa loves Goldie, her
pet _ish.

This busy buzzing b_ _
is chasing Daddy Pig.

George has found a
wriggly _orm

Mummy Pig has spotted
a cra_ at the beach.

Answer: 1. f-ish, 2. b-ee, 3. w-orm, 4. cra-b

Rabbit to the Rescue!

Join the dots to finish the picture of Miss Rabbit's helicopter. Then colour it in, so Miss Rabbit can fly off to her next emergency.

Wop!

Wop!

Wop!

Holiday Time

Yippee! Peppa and George are going on holiday. What should they pack? Draw lines to put each item in their suitcases.

Up in the Sky

Peppa, George and their family are jetting off on holiday. Look at all the lovely patterns the aeroplane has made in the sky! Draw over the patterns on the page. Then, use your hand to draw more patterns in the air.

Can you pretend to be an aeroplane whooshing through the sky?

Princess Tea Party

Peppa and her friends are having a very special tea party. Look at the picture of all the colourful things on the table. Colour in the circles as you spot each colour.

What is your favourite food on the table?

purple   pink   orange   yellow   red   green

Moon Maze

Five, four, three, two, one . . . BLAST OFF!
Help Grampy Rabbit zoom through space on
his rocket and land on the moon.

How many
stars does
he pass on
the way?

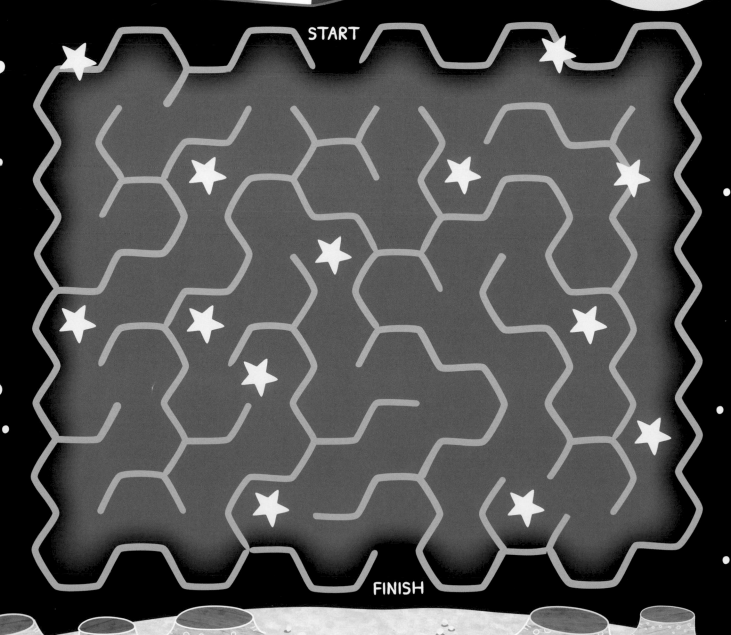

START

FINISH

Peppa's Shopping List

Can you help Peppa find everything on her shopping list? As you find each item in the supermarket, draw it in her trolley.

Peppa's Shopping List

 1 tin of pineapple

 1 tin of asparagus

 2 tins of mushrooms

1 packet of pasta

2 tins of tomatoes

Circus Tricks

Introducing the one and only amazing juggling elephant . . . Emily! Use the little picture to help you colour in Peppa and Emily on stage at the circus.

Balloon Shapes

Draw lines to match the shapes to the right balloons.

1

2

3

4

5

Which balloon do you think is George's favourite?

a

b

c

d

e

Answers: 1. e, 2. c, 3. d, 4. a, 5. b. George's favourite is the dinosaur balloon.

45

Best Fishes!

Peppa and George have chosen their favourite fish at the aquarium.

Which fish are your favourites?

How many of Peppa's favourite fish can you spot in the tank?

How many of George's favourite fish can you find in the tank?

Answers: There are five of Peppa's favourite fish and seven of George's favourite fish in the tank.

Giant Sandcastle

Look at these sandcastle sequences and draw in the missing castles.

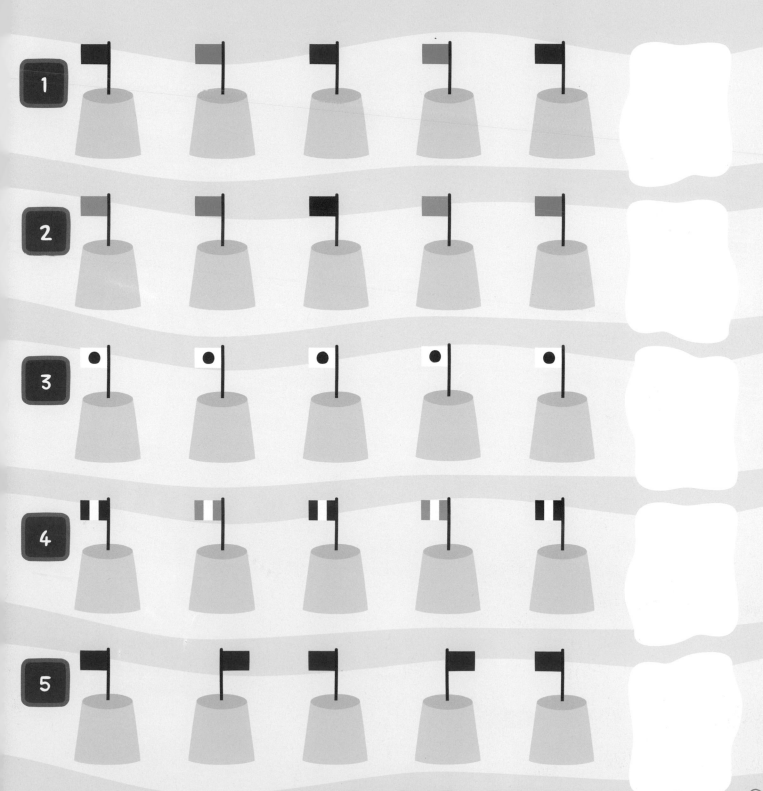

Grandpa Pig's Noisy Singalong Train

Roll a dice and take a trip on Grandpa's little train, singing the songs as you go. The first one to reach the engine carriage is the winner.

START

SING: "The piggies on the train go, 'Snort, snort, snort!'"

SING: "The ponies on the train go, 'Neigh, neigh, neigh!'"

SING: "The wolves on the train go, 'Arh-woo, arh-woo, arh-woo!'"

SING: "The dinosaurs on the train go, 'Grrr, grr, grr!'"

SING: "The daddies on the train go, 'Faster, faster, faster!'"

When you land on a carriage, sing the song. For example,

"The piggies on the train go, 'Snort, snort, snort. Snort, snort, snort. Snort, snort, snort.'

The piggies on the train go, 'Snort, snort, snort.' All day long."

SING: "The sheep on the train go, 'Baa, baa, baa!'"

SING: "The cats on the train go, 'Meow, meow, meow!'"

SING: "The dogs on the train go, 'Woof, woof, woof!'"

SING: "The foxes on the train go, 'Yap, yap, yap!'"

YOU'VE FINISHED!

SING: "Grandpa's little train goes, Choo, choo, choo!"

49

Bedtime Story

It's night-time, and Peppa and George should be asleep.
"Dine-saw! Grrr!" growls George, playing with his toys.
"George!" cries Peppa. "Go back to sleep! Night-time is for sleeping, not playing."

George hops back into bed and Peppa tucks him in.
"I'll tell you a bedtime story," says Peppa.
"Grunt! Grunt!" snorts George.
"Once upon a time there was a little pig," begins Peppa. "His name was Georgie Pig."

"Georgie Pig was off to make his fortune," Peppa goes on. "Soon he came to a forest and inside the forest was a little house. He knocked on the door, but nobody answered."

"Georgie Pig walked inside the house anyway. Inside was –"
Peppa thinks for a moment – "a bowl of porridge! Georgie Pig was very hungry, so he ate it all up! Yum, yum, yum!"

"But, just as he finished, Baby Bear walked in and said, 'Hey! Did you eat my magic porridge?' Georgie said, 'Yes,' and Baby Bear said, 'That was magic porridge! It will make you grow very big!'"

"Suddenly there was a rumbling noise and Georgie began to grow! He grew and grew and grew . . . until he was taller than all of the trees."

"The end," says Peppa. "Are you sleepy now, George?"
"No!" replies George.
"OK," says Peppa, "I'll do a little bit more . . ."

"Baby Bear told Georgie Pig there was a box of golden treasure at the end of the world, but it was too far for him to go, as he was so little. So Georgie said, 'I will carry you there,' and he walked to the end of the world . . . THUD, THUD, THUD!"

Peppa stops the story and says,
"Are you sleepy yet, George?"
"No," replies George.

"Georgie walked and he walked and he walked," Peppa carries on. "Through forests, across mountains, across seas – to the end of the world, where he found a big box of treasure and . . . a dragon."

"Ooooh!" gasps George, excitedly. "Roarrr!"

"Luckily," continues Peppa, "it was a very friendly dragon and he told Georgie he could have the treasure. But then Georgie began to shrink back to his normal size."

"Uh-oh!" says George.

"'How will we get back home?' said Baby Bear. 'I'll fly you,' said the dragon. So Georgie and Baby Bear hopped on to the dragon's back and flew all the way back to the little house. And then . . . it's the end."

Peppa yawns and looks over at George, who is fast asleep. Then she falls asleep, too.

Daddy Pig comes into the bedroom and finds George asleep in bed and Peppa asleep on the floor.

"Peppa, what are you doing out of bed?" asks Daddy Pig. "Night-time is for sleeping, not playing!"

Daddy Pig picks Peppa up and tucks her into bed.

"Night-night, my little piggies," he whispers to Peppa and George.

"Sweet dreams."

Story-time Fun

What can you remember about Peppa's bedtime story for George? See if you can answer these questions to retell the story.

1 Where did Georgie Pig find the little house?

a in the sea **b** in the forest

2 What magic food did Georgie Pig eat?

a porridge **b** jelly

3 What happened straight after Georgie Pig ate the food?

a he got smaller **b** he got bigger

4 Who did Georgie Pig carry to find the treasure?

a Baby Bear **b** Baby Goat

5 Who flew Georgie Pig back to the little house?

a Miss Rabbit in her helicopter

b the dragon

Answers: 1. b, 2. a, 3. b, 4. a, 5. b

Big and Small

In the story, Georgie Pig grew very big! Look at these objects, then draw a circle around the bigger one in each box.

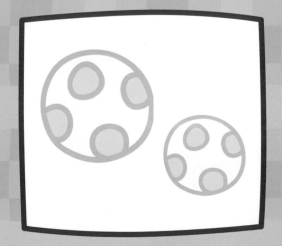

Dine-saw Bookmark

Ask a grown-up to help you follow the instructions to make your very own dinosaur bookmark.

You will need:
* scissors
* green cardboard
* white cardboard
* glue
* black pen
* yellow pen

What to do:

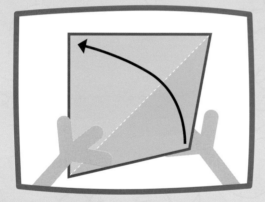

1 Start with a square piece of green card. Fold it in half diagonally to form a triangle.

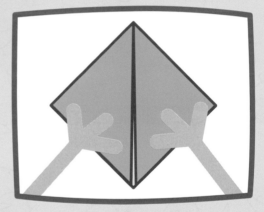

3 Next, fold the top left corner down to the bottom to form a square.

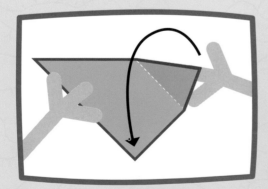

2 Lay the triangle down so the folded line is at the top, then fold the top right corner down to the bottom.

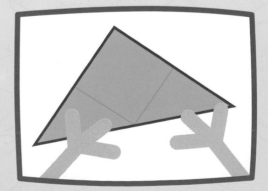

4 Unfold the two flaps, then turn the triangle around so the folded line is at the bottom.

58

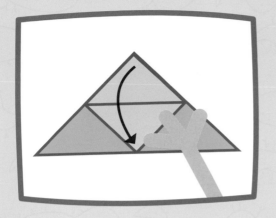

5 Fold a triangle flap down from the top point, as shown.

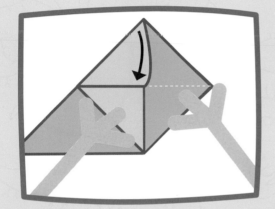

6 Fold the bottom right corner towards the middle and tuck it behind the triangle flap.

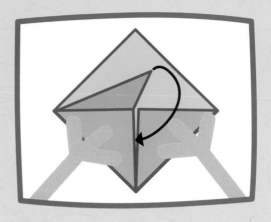

7 Fold and tuck the bottom left corner in the same way.

8 Cut out two small circles of white card for eyes, draw a black dot in the middle of each one and glue them on. Then draw yellow teeth and glue those on, as shown.

9 Now your dinosaur bookmark is ready to use. Grrr! Don't let it eat your book before you finish reading it!

59

Whoosh!

Draw yourself on the dragon's back with Georgie Pig and Baby Bear. Then colour in the picture and soar through the sky!

Night-night!

Here's a poem about Peppa and George. When you see a picture, say the word next to it in the key.

Key

bed

Peppa

George

Mr Dinosaur

Teddy

Mummy Pig

Daddy Pig

Hop into [bed], everyone's ready.

[Mummy Pig] and [George], [Mr Dinosaur] and [Teddy].

Snuggled under the covers and tucked up tight,

[Mummy Pig] and [Daddy Pig] kiss all goodnight.

Look out for these other great Peppa Pig books!

Peppa's Fishy Friends

Best Friends
A lift-the-flap book

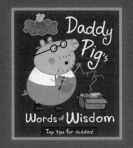
Daddy Pig's Words of Wisdom
Top tips for daddies!

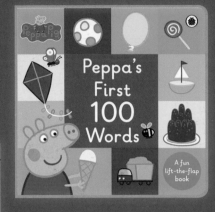
Peppa's First 100 Words
A fun lift-the-flap book

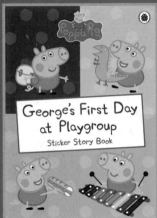
George's First Day at Playgroup
Sticker Story Book

SUPER STICKERS
Over 1000 stickers inside!

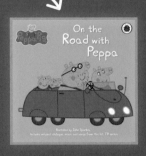
Peppa's Gym Class

Fairy Tales!
Sticker Book

CD and audio downloads

Once Upon a Time

On the Road with Peppa

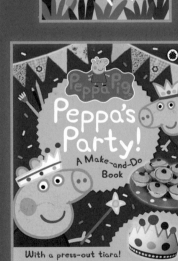
Peppa's Party!
A Make-and-Do Book
With a press-out tiara!

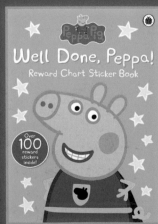
Well Done, Peppa!
Reward Chart Sticker Book
Over 100 reward stickers inside!

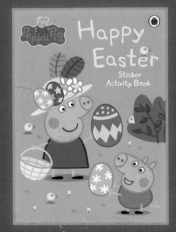
Happy Easter
Sticker Activity Book

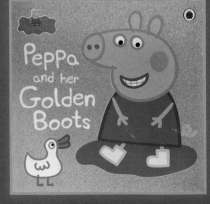
Peppa and her Golden Boots

My Best Teacher

Slow Down, George!